Cows are Ve

'A lovely retelling of the Dubs v. culchies
theme, the city girl who hates the country
(until she goes there)'
Irish Independent

'A self-proclaimed genius, with a sharp tongue
and an honours degree in retort, Michelle is a
delightfully sassy and street-wise character'
The Irish Times

'This is simply a very funny book'
Sunday Tribune

'A delightful read'
Books Ireland

Siobhán Parkinson

lives in Dublin with her woodturner husband
Roger Bennett, and son Matthew, who acts as her
personal proofreader. She is the author of many
books for children and has won several awards for
her work, including the Bisto Book of the Year
award for *Sisters ... no way!* and Bisto Merit awards
for *The Moon King* and *Four Kids, Three Cats, Two
Cows, One Witch (maybe)*.

Her books have also been translated into many lan-
guages, such as Latvian, French, German, Japanese,
Italian, Portuguese and Spanish. Siobhán's other
book in the Red Flag series, *Animals Don't Have
Ghosts*, tells the story of what happens when Sinéad
and Dara visit Michelle in the city.

COWS ARE VEGETARIANS

SIOBHÁN PARKINSON
Illustrated by Catherine Henderson

THE O'BRIEN PRESS
DUBLIN

This edition first published in 2001 by The O'Brien Press Ltd,
20 Victoria Road, Dublin 6, Ireland.
Tel: +353 1 4923333; Fax: +353 1 4922777
E-mail: books@obrien.ie
Website: www.obrien.ie
Reprinted 2003.

ISBN 0-86278-694-0

British Library Cataloguing-in-Publication Data
A catalogue reference for this title is available from
the British Library.

2 3 4 5 6 7
03 04 05 06 07

The O'Brien Press receives
assistance from

Editing, typesetting, layout, design: The O'Brien Press Ltd
Printing: Cox & Wyman Ltd

Still for Karyn
And this time also for Oisín

CONTENTS

1

The Downstairs Bedroom

My name's Michelle and I'm a Dub. That means I'm from Dublin. Dublin is the capital of Ireland, and it's the best and everyone else is a culchie.

I live with my ma and my nana. Most of the time my ma's all right. But sometimes she gets these ideas, see. And this is the story about what happened when she got one of those ideas of hers.

It started with the wellingtons. I mean, wellingtons! Red ones. I like red. I like red because it's a colour that says, 'Hey, look at me, I'm red!' I like red shoes. I like red tops. But not red wellingtons. Not wellingtons in *any* colour. Not even rainbow wellingtons. Wellingtons are for culchies.

'Who're the wellingtons for, Ma?' I said, though it was obvious it had to be me, because no one else in our family has feet that size.

'They're for you!' said Ma, and I knew from the way she said it that she meant, 'You'd better like them.'

'What for?' I asked.

'For your trip to the country,' said Ma, with this frozen sort of smile on her face, like someone was taking her photograph.

'The country? Me? No, Ma. You don't understand. I don't *do* the country.'

'You'll have a great time, Michelle,' Ma said. 'We're going to go down over Easter to see your cousins, Sinéad and Dara.'

Sinéad's OK, only she's a bit of a know-all. Dara is her little brother and he's a baby. He's not even six yet.

'We're going, Michelle,' said Ma, in

that voice she uses when she's not going to argue. I hate it when she doesn't argue. I like arguing.

So we went. We have this car that Ma is dead proud of because it's eight years old and it passed its test. I'm eight years old too, and she doesn't seem to be half as proud of me, and I'm always passing tests. Every Friday we have a spelling test and I always pass. Nearly always. Well, sometimes. More often than I pass the sum tests, anyway, only they're on Wednesdays.

The journey was dead boring. Everything was green, all grass and trees and stuff, and there were no shopping centres or car parks or playgrounds or anything nice

and friendly and human-looking like that. And there were all these wild animals in the fields, cows and sheep and horses and every sort of thing. I bet they'd eat you if they got half a chance.

The further we got from Dublin, the worse it got, and the greener, and the fields started to have little stony walls around them. I suppose it's to keep the wild animals from jumping out and eating the people going past in their cars.

After about ten hours we got to Sinéad and Dara's house. It was stuck all by itself out in the middle of a field. They call it a garden, because it has a gate and a flowerbed by the front door, but it's a field all right. I'd hate that, living in a field. No neighbours, nothing, no clubs or shops or street-lights. Just lots of green stuff.

Anyway, Sinéad and Dara were waiting for us. Dara ran away when he saw the

car coming, because he's only a baby, but Sinéad came and said hello and gave my ma a kiss and a hug like a proper little girl. I never kiss people, I think it's soppy, but you could see my ma thought Sinéad was wonderful, giving her a kiss and all.

Then we went into the house and Sinéad said I was going to sleep in her room, and I thought that'd be OK. At home, me and my ma share a room, and it's cool, because Ma comes to bed real late and I usually wake up and then we have chats. But I thought it'd be nice to share a room with Sinéad. We could have midnight feasts and pillow-fights and all those things kids in books do that my ma isn't interested in.

But we went down this narrow sort of hallway and there were no stairs.

'Where's the stairs?' I asked.

'We haven't got stairs,' Sinéad said, proudly, as if not having stairs was something special.

'So where are the bedrooms, then?' I asked.

'Here,' said Sinéad, and she flung open the door into a downstairs bedroom.

It looked very weird, I thought. You looked out the window, and there everything was, that field and everything, real

close. Anyone could stick their head in the window. I didn't like it one little bit.

'Is this a cottage?' I asked. I've read about cottages. They're little houses in the country with no upstairs and there's usually a witch living in them.

'It's a bungalow,' said Sinéad.

Ooh, I thought, a *bung*alow. Well, la-di-da to you, Miss Know-all Sinéad.

But I had a good bounce on the bed anyway. I gave it eight out of ten for bounce. My bed at home is a bit old and only gets about six out of ten.

Just as I was testing out the bed, what did I see, only a wild animal coming up to the window. I told you that garden was really a field.

'Sinéad,' I yelped. 'Sinéad, there's a wild animal out there!'

That got old Sinéad going all right.

She ran right over to the window.

'That's not a wild animal,' she said, laughing. The cheek of her, laughing! 'That's Henry.'

Henry. Well, what sort of a name for a wild animal is that?

Henry was this huge cow. Next thing, Sinéad opened the window to talk to him, and he stuck his big head in the window. He was *chewing* all the time.

'Hey, Sinéad!' I yelled. 'Don't let him stick his head in like that. He's ... he's *slobbering* all down the wallpaper. It's disgusting!'

'Henry's not a he,' said Sinéad. I mean, what a time to be correcting my grammar! 'She's a cow, and she's very friendly.'

Well, I could see that he was a cow, and he didn't look a bit friendly to me. I didn't like the way he was chewing. I could see he was planning to eat the curtains.

'Henry is a boy's name,' I said.

'Not in this case,' said Sinéad, and I swear, she was stroking the cow's face. 'It's short for Henrietta.'

'Don't touch him, Sinéad,' I shouted. 'He'll bite you. He'll eat you!'

'She won't eat me. Cows are vegetarians.'

Vegetarians, right – as if that made any difference.

'Who cares what star-sign he is? He can still eat you,' I said.

'Vegetarian isn't a star-sign,' said Sinéad. 'It means not eating meat.'

'I know what it means,' I said, 'but he can still eat you. It doesn't matter about his religion.'

I was thinking about those people in

India, I suppose. The ones that only eat vegetables because meat is against their religion.

Sinéad said cows didn't have any religion. I said they could if they wanted to. She said they wouldn't want to. I said, how would she know. It was one of those arguments that start out being quite fun but then start to get stupid.

In the end, Sinéad said she had to go and take Henry out of the garden and put him back in his field. I didn't point out that the garden was a field anyway, as far

as I could see, because I was glad to think that he wouldn't be able to stick his head in the window. I wouldn't be able to sleep if I thought there was a wild animal outside, waiting for us to go to sleep so he could get a good bite at us.

'Don't mind her,' I heard Sinéad saying to the cow when she was leading him away. 'She's only down from Dublin.'

Well!

2

The Maternity Hospital

The next day, Uncle Seán said we should eat up our breakfasts quickly and come down to the maternity hospital. Uncle Seán is Sinéad's da and Aunty Peggy is her ma, and they're dead nice, except that they wear these big hairy woolly jumpers that smell of farmyard. That's because they're farmers. They don't do it on purpose.

I knew he didn't mean a real maternity hospital, because it was perfectly obvious that there was nothing as civilised as a hospital anywhere near the farm. I knew it was some sort of a joke, but I couldn't work out what it meant. I didn't let on, though, because that would only be giving in to those culchies, the way they think they're so superior to the Dubs.

'OK,' I said.

I picked up my cornflakes bowl and drank the last of the milk out of it. I'm not allowed to do that at home, but my ma wasn't up yet, so there was no one to stop me, though I noticed Sinéad looking at me in horror. She's aghast, I thought.

'Are you aghast, Sinéad?' I asked.

'She's not a ghost,' said Dara.

'Oh, I think she is,' I said. 'She's a ghost. She died in the night because Henry ate her up, and now she's a ghost. She's a shadow of her former self.'

Dara looked worried for a minute, about Sinéad being eaten and turning into a shadow, but he could see well enough that his sister was sitting there munching cornflakes in a very bodily sort of way.

'You're joking,' he said, as if he'd made a great discovery.

Then he picked up his own cornflakes bowl and he slurped his milk, and Sinéad looked even more aghast, and me and Dara had a little giggle at her. She didn't like that. I felt a bit sorry for her for a moment, but then I remembered how she said cows couldn't have a religion even if they wanted to, and I told myself she deserved it.

'I don't know what you're going to do about your feet,' Sinéad said to me as we got ready to go out on the farm. She puts on this grown-up voice sometimes. It drives me wild. 'I don't suppose you have any wellies.'

'Of course I have,' I said. I never thought I'd be glad to be the proud owner of one pair of wellington boots, red.

That knocked the wind out of her sails all right, and I could see that she thought my wellies were very smart. Which they are. For wellies.

The maternity hospital was a sheep-shed, full of sheep and lambs. They were making the most terrible racket, all baa-ing and maa-ing. I always thought that the lambs say 'maa' because they're

calling for their mas, and the mother
sheep say 'baa' because they're calling
for their babies, but it turns out that they
all say something that's sort of halfway
between 'maa' and 'baa' and they say it
an awful lot of the time, very loudly.
You'd get a headache listening to the lot

of them. And it's pretty smelly in the sheep-shed, too. Smells of sheep pooh.

The sheep-shed was all divided up into these little sort of separate bedrooms, with bales of straw. I was hanging over the top of one of the straw bales, looking in at a sheep, when I noticed that it was acting sort of strange. It was lying down in a corner and it looked as if it was trying to get through the straw wall, it was pushing up so close against it.

'Look at that sheep, there,' I said to Sinéad, pointing at it with a straw. 'It's trying to get through the wall.'

'Oh good heavens!' yelled Sinéad.

I couldn't see what the fuss was about. I didn't think there was much chance that the sheep really would get through the wall. But anyway, Sinéad leapt up off the bale of straw she was sitting on and she went running off looking for someone.

She came back a minute later, and her mother was running after her.

'Well spotted, Michelle,' said Aunty Peggy.

I hadn't a clue what she was talking about.

Aunty Peggy took a leap over the straw bales into the little cubicle where the sheep was, and she sat down on the ground beside it and started talking to it in whispers.

'Good girl,' she was saying, 'good girl.'

'What's happening?' I asked Sinéad.

'She's having a baby,' said Sinéad.

'What! Your mother is having a *baby*! In a *sheep*-shed! Oh, we have to get the doctor, quick!'

'Not my mother, silly – the sheep.'

I felt a bit stupid, but it wasn't my fault. Sinéad should have said 'having a lamb', not 'having a baby'. Sheep don't have babies. Even I know that.

'I knew that,' I said. 'But do we not have to get the doctor anyway? I mean, the vet.'

'No, no, she'll be fine,' said Sinéad.

'Is he going to have it right here?' I asked.

'Yes, of course,' said Sinéad. 'She.'

I could feel myself going green. You wouldn't think that's possible, but it is. You get this green feeling in your stomach, and you can feel it in your face as well, as if your skin is gone sort of mouldy and luminous.

'Oh dear,' I said. 'I think I have to leave.'

I went outside to get some fresh air. Sinéad came out after me, and Dara too, and I could see that they were having a good laugh at me. Well, I mean, they're used to the smell of sheep pooh and people having babies all over the place. Sheep, I mean, having lambs. But I'm a city girl, I am.

33

3

The Cow Parlour

Sinéad said we should have a race, then, in the next field. I said OK, because I knew I could win the race, because I'm the fastest.

Sinéad won, but that's only because my wellingtons were new and I hadn't been training for running in wellies. You can't just do that sort of thing straight off. You have to practise. But I didn't say any of that. I let Sinéad think she'd won fair and square, even though I was the guest and

the polite thing would have been for her to let me win.

I did say I had run slowly, though, so that Dara wouldn't be left too far behind, because he's only little.

'No you didn't,' Sinéad said. 'You ran as hard as you could.'

'How do you know?' I asked. 'You've never seen me run before. You don't know how fast I am.'

'I could hear you breathing,' she said, as if that makes any difference. I breathe all the time. What does she do, I'd like to know – take in air through her pores or something?

Plus, I had to run around the cowpats. Sinéad just ran right through them. She doesn't care about getting cow pooh on her wellies, because she's a culchie and anyway her wellies are old. But I couldn't be getting old mucky stuff on my nice new red wellingtons. My mother would kill me.

After that, we went on a visit to Uncle Dan. I never met Uncle Dan before. He's Sinéad and Dara's grand-uncle. That means he's like a grandfather, only an uncle. I think he might be my grand-uncle too.

Uncle Dan lives in a proper cottage – you know, with those cloudy sort of walls and hay on the roof.

'It's not hay,' said Dara, 'it's straw.'

'Same thing,' I said.

'No it's not,' said Dara. He was getting to be a bit cheeky. I blame Sinéad. He picks it up from her. If I had a little brother, I wouldn't give him bad example like that.

'Well, what's the difference?' I asked, but of course he couldn't say, so I was right as usual.

There were hens running around out-side Uncle Dan's door. When we came up close to the cottage, Sinéad whooshed the hens away by clapping her hands, and they all went off, squawking and flapping.

I thought that was pretty cool, the way she was able to frighten away the hens. Sinéad's OK really, when she isn't show-ing off and winning races by cheating.

Uncle Dan's door was cut in two, and the top half was open, so we could look in over the bottom half and see him asleep in his chair with the newspaper over his face.

We opened the bottom half of the door and tiptoed into the kitchen. It smelt of potatoes in there.

We tried to be very quiet so as not to wake Uncle Dan up, but then we got bored, so in the end we decided we would cough gently, to see if he was really asleep. That woke him up all right, and he snatched the newspaper off his nose and said: 'Musha, is it yourselves?'

He talks country, like somebody on one of those old radio programmes my nana listens to.

'It is,' I said. 'Who else would it be?' I was getting the hang of this country talk myself.

'And who are you?' he asked me.

'I'm Michelle and I'm from Dublin.'

'A jackeen, is it?' he said, sitting up straight now and taking notice.

Jackeen is what culchies call Dublin people because they don't know that the proper word is Dub.

'And I suppose you're all very hungry and thirsty after that long walk over the fields,' said Uncle Dan.

I liked him. He doesn't mess about like other grown-ups, asking you what your teacher's name is and stupid stuff like that. As if they're going to know your teacher if you tell them her name.

'It wasn't a very long walk,' I said, because I always try to be truthful when I can, 'but we're hungry and thirsty anyway.'

So Uncle Dan got out a tin of biscuits that said USA Assortment on the lid,

only they were really custard creams, and a large bottle of red lemonade, and we had a little banquet there in his kitchen. The custard creams weren't bad. I never ate them before. I think they must be country biscuits. One of the hens flew up and landed on the top of the bottom half of the door, and I didn't even mind.

After we'd had our banquet, Uncle Dan whooshed the hens away again and we went out into the yard, because Patrick was bringing the cows in for milking.

Patrick is Uncle Dan's son and he is a cow-farmer. He owns Henry.

Uncle Dan wanted to show us the milking-parlour.

'This isn't a parlour,' I said, looking around. 'It's just a big cow-shed. A parlour has to have a carpet and a sofa.'

'Not this sort of parlour,' said Uncle Dan, which goes to show that country people haven't a clue. Even nice ones, like Uncle Dan. But I didn't bother to argue. Country people always have to be right, even if they're wrong. So you're as well off not arguing in the first place.

4

The Lamb in the Kitchen

One day when we got home from our adventures on the farm, Uncle Seán was in the kitchen, stirring his famous soup. When the lambs are being born Uncle Seán and Aunty Peggy are too busy to cook much, so every Sunday Uncle Seán makes this really huge pot of soup and they eat it every day for the rest of the week. It's called Uncle Seán's famous soup on account of being famous in three counties. I think that is just Uncle Seán's little joke, but it's delicious anyway, even if it isn't really famous.

We were about halfway through our soup when I heard this weird sound in the kitchen. I looked around, but nobody else seemed to notice. Maybe they're used to that sort of thing in the country, but it seemed very strange to me, because what I was hearing was a lamb bleating in its little sad lamb's voice.

It sounded very close, as if it was actually in the kitchen. There it was again, 'Baa-aa-aa,' and it was definitely in the room.

I put my spoon down and I said, 'Am I imagining it, people, or is there a lamb in this room?'

'No,' said Uncle Seán. 'And yes. You're not and there is.'

Everyone went on eating the famous

soup, as if having a lamb in the kitchen was the most normal thing in the world. That's culchies for you, I thought.

'It's a pet,' said Aunty Peggy, when she saw how gobsmacked I looked.

'A *pet*?' I thought she must be joking me.

'Yes, a pet lamb. We usually have one or two every year. He lives over there.' She pointed to a box under the cooker.

(They call it a range, in the country. It's always on, even when they're not cooking on it.)

The woman next door to us in Dublin has about twenty-five million cats, and I had two goldfish once but I think they ate each other. Anyway, they disappeared. But those are the kinds of animals you are *supposed* to have for pets. Not lambs.

Ma is always telling me I am too 'pass-remarkable', and I shouldn't always be telling people they're being stupid, even if they are. So I decided I would say something nice, even though I secretly thought they were being very stupid.

'That's *terrific*,' I said in my most enthusiastic voice. I said it loudly and clearly, so Ma would get the message that I wasn't saying anything about it being stupid to make a pet of a lamb. But she didn't notice.

'Would you like to feed him?' Aunty Peggy asked.

'OK,' I said, because I had finished my famous soup by now, and I was trying to be helpful because Aunty Peggy is so nice. 'Where do you keep the lamb-food?'

I thought it would come in a tin, like cat-food, and that I would just have to spoon it out into a little dish.

Sinéad and Dara started laughing at me again. I wanted to tell them about not being pass-remarkable, but Aunty Peggy said, 'Actually, it's a bottle that you give him.'

'Oh!' I said.

She handed me a baby's bottle full of milk. I shook my head and put my hands behind my back, because I knew she had to be joking me and I wasn't going to fall for it. Sinéad and Dara were snorting like pigs by now.

'You do it, Sinéad,' I said then. That'd stop her laughing. See how *she* liked being made to look like an eejit.

'OK,' said Sinéad, and she took the bottle and picked up the little lamb. She stuck the bottle in his gob, and sure enough the lamb started guzzling the milk like crazy. Amazing!

'Hey!' I said. 'He really does drink out of a baby's bottle.'

'Of course he does,' said Dara.

'Well, how was I to know?' I said, and I stuck out my tongue at him when the grown-ups were busy serving out the dessert. He stuck out his tongue back, which I thought was good, for a baby.

'Do you want a go now, Michelle?' asked Sinéad, holding out the bottle to me. 'It's a lovely feeling, feeding him.'

She can be very soppy, Sinéad.

'No, thanks,' I said.

I bet he'd bite me if I tried to feed him. I bet he'd suck the bottle so hard he'd swallow it and my hand would get stuck in his mouth and get all mangled up in his teeth and I'd have to go to hospital and have the lamb surgically removed. I'd never be able to use my hand again or play the guitar and that would be the end of me being a rock star when I grow up.

'I don't *do* pet lambs,' I added. 'I'm from Dublin.'

But in the end I tried, and I was great at it, I was.

5

Adventure in the Night

I woke up in the middle of the night. I could hear Sinéad breathing in the dark. She doesn't suck air in through her pores at all. She breathes like a normal person. Which isn't to say that she *is* normal, of course.

It was very dark, much darker than it gets in Dublin, and very quiet. I have a nice friendly street-light outside my window at home, so it's never really dark in my room, and there are always loads of cars going by, making comfortable noises.

All that dark and quiet can't be healthy, I think. I mean, how do people sleep with it?

It was nice listening to someone breathing, even if it was only soppy old Sinéad. But after a while, I began to hear something else, apart from Sinéad's breathing. A soft bleating sound in the distance. The pet lamb, I thought. (Larry, they called him. Very country.)

Stupid animal, I thought, whingeing in the night, like a baby. Stupid and annoying. I put my pillow over my ears, but still I could hear him, crying away, and I couldn't stop thinking about him.

Once I started to think about Larry, lying in his box under the range in the kitchen, not able to sleep because of all the dark and the quiet, I went all sort of soft. Poor little thing, I thought. He misses his ma. He must be lonely.

I don't usually think like that. It was only because it was the middle of the night and I was feeling a bit lonely myself.

In the end, I decided I'd better go and pay Larry a little visit, to make sure he was all right, and to see if I could shut him up. I rolled out of bed, very quietly so as not to wake Sinéad, and I padded up the long hallway to the kitchen.

I didn't bring my slippers with me, so I had to curl my toes when I got to the kitchen, because the floor was cold. I put on the kitchen light, and there was Larry standing up in his box, looking all lost and wobbly.

'You poor ould eejit,' I said, speaking in country so he would understand me.

'Baa-aa-aa,' he said.

I bent down and lifted him up in my arms. I bet you think lambs are all soft and fluffy, like in a Comfort ad. Well, they're not. They're sort of hard and pointy and their fur is rough and springy. He was trembling, and I could feel his little heart, beating far too fast.

I was starting to get a bit cold, in my nightdress and bare feet. All I wanted was to get back into bed, but I couldn't leave the poor little thing there, bleating away sadly in the dark. I don't know what came over me, but anyway I said to him, 'Come on. Let's get warm.'

I snapped off the kitchen light and I flew down the hallway again, to the bedroom. Sinéad was still asleep.

I was really freezing at this stage, so I got in under the covers very quickly with Larry in my arms. He was still bleating a little bit, but I could see he was much happier now than he had been in his lonely old box.

I think I must have drifted off to sleep then, because the next thing I knew, Aunty Peggy was standing over me, shaking my shoulder and saying, 'Michelle, Michelle!'

Sinéad was standing beside her, saying 'I *told* you,' in that smug, know-all voice of hers. 'I told you.'

'Have you got Larry in bed with you, Michelle?' Aunty Peggy asked. 'What on earth … Has he piddled in the bed?'

'What!' I sat bolt upright. What a thought! Lamb-piddle in my bed. I started patting the sheet, to see if it was damp, but it wasn't. 'Do you mean he's not house-trained?' I was shocked. What sort of people were they?

'House-trained!' said Aunty Peggy, and she started to laugh. She laughed so hard she had to sit down on the end of my bed to get over it. At last she said, 'You don't house-train lambs, Michelle.'

Well, how was I supposed to know that?

'But I thought you said he was a pet.'

'Yes, but …' Aunty Peggy went off into

another gale of laughter, and Sinéad was laughing too, fit to burst. I wished she *would* burst. That'd make a nice mess in her bed. Much worse than lamb-piddle.

'A pet lamb isn't a pet like a puppy or a kitten, Michelle,' Aunty Peggy said. 'It means a lamb whose mother has died, and who needs to be fed from a bottle, that's all. Not a pet like an animal from a pet-shop.'

'I knew that,' I said, still holding on to Larry, but I knew no one believed me. I could feel myself going red. I'm not usually stupid. Actually, I am mega-clever. It's just that they do things all wrong in the country, and how could you expect me to understand? I think they just do it to confuse city people, which is very mean of them.

'Here, give him to me,' Aunty Peggy

said. 'I'll put him back in his box. And you two get back to sleep now, like good girls.'

She turned off the light. I was glad. I didn't want Sinéad looking at me and sniggering.

Aunty Peggy tucked us both in and kissed us good night. I didn't mind being kissed because it was dark and no one could see. Off she went then, with Larry bleating in her arms.

'Michelle,' said Sinéad after a while.

'What?' I asked, lying on my back and trying to see the ceiling through all the darkness. I didn't really want to talk to Sinéad. I could just imagine what she would say: how could I think a pet lamb was a pet like a kitten, and all this stuff.

'Sorry I laughed,' Sinéad said. 'I wasn't really laughing at you. It's just that ...' And off she went again, laughing like mad.

This time, I laughed too. I did it mainly to show her I wasn't offended, but really, I suppose, there was a funny side to it as well.

'What did you have to call your mother for, though?' I asked then.

'Well,' said Sinéad, 'see, I woke up, and you were asleep and I felt lonely, so I thought I'd go and see how Larry was, but he wasn't there. So then I went and

woke up my mam, because I thought maybe someone had kidnapped him. That's how come she was up.'

'Kidnapped! You thought someone might have *kidnapped* Larry!' I mean, who would want to kidnap a lamb that can't even feed itself?

'Well … ,' said Sinéad.

I could have had a good laugh at her. But I decided I wouldn't. I thought I would be very gracious and not make her feel stupid. I can be super-kind sometimes, when I am in the mood.

But she knew herself. 'That was a bit stupid, wasn't it?' she said.

'Yeah,' I said. 'But you do think silly things in the middle of the night, don't you? And taking Larry into my bed was kind of stupid too.'

I don't know what made me say that.

I didn't know I could be *that* kind.

'We're two right eejits, aren't we?' said Sinéad.

'Ah no,' I said. 'We're just a bit – ehh – inexperienced.'

'Yeah,' said Sinéad. 'That's it. Inexperienced.'

And then we both fell asleep.

6

Home

We had to go home then, because Ma's holidays were over and she had to get back to work.

The weird thing was, I didn't really want to leave. I was starting to get used to the country, even though I still think it's not a patch on the city. Not a patch.

Ma said Sinéad and Dara could come and visit us in the summer, and we could ring each other at weekends if we wanted to. So I said that would have to do, and

Sinéad said we didn't have any choice, and Dara said he didn't like using the phone. I hadn't been planning to ring Dara up, but it was kind of nice that he thought I would want to speak to him as well, wasn't it? I suppose he'll grow out of being a baby.

So we packed everything up, and we went and said goodbye to Uncle Dan, and he gave us half a sack of potatoes and three big cabbages to take back to Dublin with us. We'll have to give the cabbages to the woman next door with all the cats, because we don't like cabbage.

And so we drove all the way back to Dublin, through all the green. I still didn't like it, but it didn't bother me so much this time. I suppose I'd got used to it.

Sinéad rang me the very next day and we started making plans. We have decided we'll have a pillow-fight when she comes to Dublin, because we never got around to it down the country. Sinéad doesn't like fighting, but I explained that a pillow-fight is only for fun. It's not real fighting. Sometimes you have to spell things out for Sinéad, but she's OK really. She can't help not being as clever as me.

I said I would take her and Dara around and show them all the tourist things because they don't know their way around Dublin and they'll need a proper Dub to show them stuff. They don't know how lucky they are to have me.

I think I'm sort of looking forward to it.

Also available in
The O'Brien Press
RED FLAG series

THE GREAT PIG ESCAPE
Linda Moller
Illustrated by Kieron Black

When the farm cat tells Runtling the
pig of his approaching fate, this little
piggy realises that the trip to market is
one he must avoid at all costs. He
warns his twelve pig-mates and
together they escape. They find an
abandoned farm, but then new own-
ers arrive and the pigs fear that their escape has been in
vain. But Nick and Polly Faraway have strange, alternative
ideas about farming and a lifestyle that might work to the
benefit of pigs and humans. Maybe there can be a happy
ending after all!

THE FIVE HUNDRED
Eilís Dillon
Illustrated by Gareth Floyd

As far back as he can remember,
Pierino has heard Luca, his father,
speak of the day when they would
own a car. At last the day arrives, and
the Fiat Five Hundred is bought and
brought home. Everyone is happy, until the car is stolen, then, *mamma mia*,
life becomes exciting!

THE FIGHT FOR PLOVER HILL
Eilís Dillon
Illustrated by Prudence Seward

John and his grandfather, Old Dan, are the only people living on Plover Hill, a little farm cut off from the rest of the valley by floodwater. They have eggs from their ducks and hens, milk and butter from the cows, and in the woods live every kind of animal and bird you ever saw: foxes, hedgehogs, squirrels, rabbits and, of course, plover. But a local property developer has his eye on Plover Hill – it would make a fine place to bring shooting parties. He challenges Dan's right to the land. Will John be able to save Plover Hill for his grandfather and for the animals for whom it is a sanctuary?

Paperback €6.34/STG£4.99/$5.95

ADAM'S STARLING
Gillian Perdue

Adam is shy and a dreamer, and when he is picked on at school by Roland and the bullies, Adam doesn't know what to do. His parents are too busy to help, so he must face this problem alone. Then a scruffy little starling follows him to school and seems to be in need of a friend, too. Will Adam find the courage at last to stand up for himself?

Paperback €6.50/STG£4.99/$7.95

BOOM CHICKA BOOM

Liz Weir

Illustrated by Josip Lizatovic

Stories old and new, with participation rhymes and playful verses, from a noted storyteller. Full of magic and drama, the book consists of the following stories: 'Going to Granny's', 'The Rabbit's Tale', 'Wee Meg Barnileg', 'Master of All Masters', 'Long Bony Finger', 'Boom Chicka Boom', 'The Tailor and the Button', 'Rathlin Fairy Tale' and 'A Riddle Story'.

Paperback €6.34/STG£4.99/$5.95

LEPRECHAUN ON THE LOOSE

Annette Kelleher

Illustrated by Phillip Morrison

Biddy Blatherskate is fed up with wet weather and minding her father's gold. When Corey, a young Australian boy visiting Ireland, stumbles on her treasure, she's willing to do a deal in exchange for a chance to visit Australia. Her father's gold for Corey's passport! But leprechauns and humans don't mix – not without a heap of trouble for all concerned! Sunburnt and in hiding, Biddy is soon fed up with Australia, too. Meanwhile, Corey's spending spree comes to nothing because no one will accept little pieces of gold instead of money. Things are looking grim for Biddy and Corey ...

Paperback €6.50/STG£4.99/$7.95

WOLFGRAN

Finbar O'Connor
Illustrated by Martin Fagan

Granny has sold her house to the three little pigs and moved into the Happy-Ever-After Home for Retirement Characters from Fairy Tales. But the Big Bad Wolf is still on her trail! Disguised as a little old lady, the wolf is causing mayhem as he prowls the city streets, swallowing anybody who gets in his way, including several very polite policemen. Hot on his heels are Chief Inspector Plonker, Sergeant Snoop and a very clever little Girl Guide in a red hood. But will they get to the wolf before he gets to Granny?

Paperback €6.50/STG£4.99/$5.95

PUGNAX AND THE PRINCESS

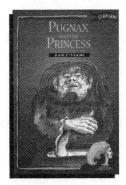

Dan Kissane
Illustrated by Brian Fitzgerald

Desperate to be wise, the King of Wisdom wants to get the Book of Riddles, but it is in the grimy hands of Prince Pugnax of Porzana. The King arranges for his daughter, Princess Ricolana, to marry the dreadful prince. She is heart-broken – but what can she do? Along comes Agamemnon who, with a little help from a strange wizard, sets out to rescue – and maybe win – the princess. But nasty Pugnax is not a man to take this kind of challenge lying down ...

Paperback €6.50/STG£4.99/$5.95

ALBERT AND THE MAGICIAN

Leon McAuley
Illustrated by Martin Fagan

When the headmaster announces that The Great Gazebo is coming to visit the school, Albert's big sister, Fionnuala, tells him awful tales about the powers of magicians, especially over seven-year-old boys. Poor Albert is terrified! When a funny-looking old man turns up at the school gate on an old banger of a bike, Albert kindly helps him carry his bags – then, horror of horrors, he discovers that this is the magician ... and now he has a *special interest in Albert!*

Paperback €6.50/STG£4.99/$7.95

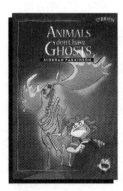

ANIMALS DON'T HAVE GHOSTS

Siobhán Parkinson
Illustrated by Cathy Henderson

Sinéad and Dara, Michelle's country cousins, come up to 'the Big Smoke' to visit Michelle and her mum. The bright lights and fast life of the city take her cousins by surprise, but Michelle delights in showing off her cosmopolitan ways! A witty and engaging account of a visit to the weird and wonderful city of Dublin, where Sinéad and Dara struggle to understand the curious local customs.

Paperback €6.50/STG£4.99/$7.95

CHARLIE HARTE AND HIS TWO-WHEELED TIGER
Frank Murphy

Charlie Harte would love to own his very own bike, but his family cannot afford to buy him one. Then he has a GREAT idea! He manages to assemble a strange-looking bike from old bits and pieces – not exactly cool, but full of character. In fact, it's so full of character that it almost begins to develop a life of its own! What is Charlie to make of all this? His unusual bike changes Charlie's life … completely!

Paperback €5.95/STG£4.50/$7.95

WALTER SPEAZLEBUD
David Donohue

Walter Speazlebud is a whizz at spelling backwards. While the other children in his class struggle to remember their spellings *forwards*, Walter can rattle off any word *backwards*. But Walter has an even better gift: the power of Noitanigami (Imagination). That means he can make people, and animals, go backwards in time. Walter inherited both skills from his favourite person: his grandfather. So when his horrible teacher, Mr Strong, starts picking on Walter, he had better watch out. And so had the even more horrible class bully, Danny Biggles. Because when Speazlebud's about, it spells elbuort (trouble) for all bullies …

Paperback €5.95/STG£4.50/$7.95

Other books from
SIOBHÁN PARKINSON, for older readers

FOUR KIDS, THREE CATS, TWO COWS, ONE WITCH (Maybe)

Beverly, a bit of a snob, cooks up a plot to visit the mysterious Lady Island off the coast. She manages to convince the somewhat cautious Elizabeth and her slob of a brother, Gerard, to go with her. A surprise companion is Kevin, the cool guy who works in the local shop. This motley crew must find ways to support each other and put up with one another's shortcomings when they become stranded on the island and encounter a very strange inhabitant.

Paperback €6.95/STG£4.99/$7.95

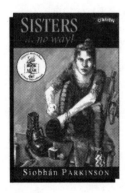

SISTERS ... NO WAY!

Cindy, a cynical teenager, still traumatised by her mother's recent death, is appalled when her father falls in love with one of her teachers. And not only that, but her teacher has two daughters – prissy, obedient types that Cindy can't stand. But if Cindy dislikes her prospective stepsisters, they think she is an absolute horror – spoiled, arrogant and atrociously rude. Is there any room for compromise?

This unique *Flipper* book allows you to read the story from two different sides – Cindy's diary and Ashling's diary.

Paperback €6.95/STG£4.99/$7.95

THE MOON KING

Ricky is put in a foster home that is full of sunshine and laughter and children of all ages. But Ricky has withdrawn from the world, and is not capable of communicating with anyone; the only words he speaks are in his mind. He has lost the ability to become part of family life. Then he finds an unusual chair in the attic, which becomes his special place. In his special chair he becomes the Moon King and finds some sense of power and inner peace. From this situation relationships slowly begin to grow, but it is not a smooth path and at times Ricky just wants to leave it all behind ...

Paperback €6.95/STG£4.99/$7.95

CALL OF THE WHALES

Over three summers, Tyke journeys with his anthropologist father to the remote and icy wilderness of the Arctic. Each summer brings short, intense friendships with the Eskimos, and adventures 'which Mum doesn't need to know about'. Tyke is saved from drowning and hypothermia, joins a bowhead whale hunt, rescues his new-found Eskimo friend, Henry, from being swept away on an ice floe, and witnesses the death of innocence with the killing of the narwhal or sea unicorn. A story that will echo in the mind long after the Northern Lights have faded from the final chapters.

Paperback €6.95/STG£4.99/$7.95

THE LOVE BEAN

Twins: they like the same things. But that can cause problems. Especially where boys are concerned. When Tito, a tall handsome African, walks into the lives of Lydia and Julia, it turns every relationship upside down. Then there's the 'twinny book' – *The Curiosity Tree*. It's about Sun'va and Eva: they're twins too. And a boy has just sailed into *their* lives, causing havoc. Romance mirrors romance, jealousy mirrors jealousy – it seems like history is repeating itself.

Paperback €6.95/STG£4.99/$7.95

Send for our full-colour catalogue